LUCIA
AND THE
LIGHT

LUCIA
AND THE
LIGHT

PHYLLIS ROOT

ILLUSTRATED BY
MARY GRANDPRÉ

CANDLEWICK PRESS
CAMBRIDGE, MASSACHUSETTS

First edition 2006

Library of Congress Cataloging-in-Publication Data is available.

Library of Congress Catalog Card Number 2006042577

ISBN-13: 978-0-7636-2296-1
ISBN-10: 0-7636-2296-6

10 9 8 7 6 5 4 3 2 1

Printed in China

This book was typeset in Caslon Antique.
The illustrations were done in pastel.

Candlewick Press
2067 Massachusetts Avenue
Cambridge, Massachusetts 02140

visit us at www.candlewick.com

For Ellen and Amelia and all the high places we've traveled
P. R.

With love to Julia Wren, for her sweet light, which
already warms my heart
M. G.

Lucia and her mother and baby brother lived with a velvet-brown cow and a milk-white cat in a little house at the foot of a mountain in the Far North. The cow gave milk, the cat slept by the fire, and the baby cooed and grew fat by the hearth. They were happy together, even when winter piled snow outside their door.

One year, the wind blew down the mountain fiercer than it ever had before. The wind screamed so loud sometimes that Lucia could not hear her mother humming as she rocked the baby by the fire. Frost covered the nail heads in the walls, and the wind that sneaked in through the cracks tossed the last of the flour in the barrel around, so that it seemed to snow inside the house as well as out.

One day, the sun did not rise over the mountaintop. And the next day and the next and the next, not a glimmer of sun shone, no matter how long Lucia watched for sunrise. Dark roosted on the land.

"Where has the light gone?" Lucia asked.

"I don't know," her mother replied. "Even the oldest tales never told of this darkness." She wrapped Lucia in her arms. "We will be each other's sun until the real sun returns," she said.

As the dark days wore on, the baby began to fret and fuss, and the cow gave less and less milk until one day she was dry as a stone. The fire smoked and shivered and refused to heat the corners of the house or bake the bread.

At last, Lucia could stand it no longer. "I will go look for the sun," she said to her mother. "Perhaps it has lost its way."

"It's too cold and dark," said her mother. "And there may be trolls. My grandmother told how when she was a girl, in the bitterest of winters, the trolls came down from the mountain and stole chickens and pigs and even a child."

Lucia shivered and hugged her baby brother close. Still she said, "Don't worry, Mama. I'll find the sun and be back in time for breakfast."

Though how could anyone tell when breakfast time was in all that dark?

"I can't let you go. We will live without the sun if we must," said Lucia's mother. The baby wailed, thin and high, and Lucia's mother shushed him.

Lucia made up her mind to do something, anything, to find the sun and bring it home again. At last, when her mother, rocking the baby, fell into a fitful sleep, Lucia put on the warmest socks, hat, and mittens that her mother had knit, pulled on boots, buttoned up her coat, and wrapped her scarf around her neck.

Into one pocket, she slipped a stale crust of bread. Into the other pocket, she put the tinderbox, for who knew when she might have need of a fire to keep her warm?

She kissed her sleeping mother's cheek, the baby's fine, soft hair, the milk-white cat, and even the cow. But when Lucia opened the door, the cat jumped from the windowsill into her hood and went out into the swirling snow with her. Lucia was glad for the company and the warmth of the milk-white cat around her neck.

Lucia strapped on her skis and set off up the mountain, where the sun used to rise. The pale light of the stars showed her the way.

Up and up the mountain Lucia skied, *shoosh, shoosh,* the air growing icier as she went.

Time seemed frozen. Lucia's fingers were sticks of ice. Surely days had passed while she pushed her skis up the mountain.

She shoved her hands into her pockets to warm them and felt something hard. Bread! The crust from the last loaf of bread her mother had baked in the fretful fire. It was as frozen as her fingers but softened as she held it in her mouth and was the sweetest thing Lucia had ever tasted. She shared bits with the milk-white cat, who mewed his thanks and licked at Lucia's mitten.

Lucia knew that as long as her legs would carry her, she would continue up the mountain.

Shoosh, shoosh. The snow squeaked beneath her skis. Her breath froze on her hair in clouds of ice. Icicles hung from the trees like frozen tears. Even the sparrows hid under their wings.

Shoooooosh. Shooooosh. The trail grew steeper. The path led Lucia into a stand of trees where even the starlight couldn't shine. Lucia's skis slipped, and she fell.

The snow was soft, almost as soft as her feather bed back home. Lucia closed her eyes. The milk-white cat nipped Lucia's chin, but Lucia kept on dreaming. If she were home, warm in her own soft bed, she would sleep and sleep and sleep. . . .

The milk-white cat nipped Lucia's chin again. "Ow!"
Lucia had almost fallen asleep in the snow—just like old Bjorn,
who had been found last winter, frozen stiff and hard as cordwood!

Lucia rubbed the heaviness from her eyes and hugged the milk-white cat, then tucked him back into her hood.

Shoosh, shoosh. Shoosh, shoosh. Shoosh, shoosh.

At last, Lucia and the milk-white cat came out of the trees and reached the top of the mountain. All they could see were rocks, ice, scraggly bushes, and the far edge of the mountain falling into darkness. Lucia's heart fell, too. Where was the sun?

Then a rock moved. And another. A rock sprouted an arm, two arms. Rocky heads with stony eyes rose up from the ground. Many heads, many eyes, all watching Lucia.

Not rocks. # TROLLS!

The trolls crowded around Lucia. Lumpy fingers poked her.

"Supper?" roared a troll with branches growing from his ears.

"No, lunch!" shouted a troll with mossy teeth.

"Breakfast!" screeched a troll with icicles hanging from his nose.

The trolls stomped their feet and screamed with laughter. The ground shook. The milk-white cat hissed.

"Please," Lucia whispered, "do you know where the sun has gone?"

"Trolls found sun sleeping!" shouted one troll.

"Wrapped sun in a blanket so sun can't get out!" shouted another.

"Now trolls never have to hide," crowed another. "Eat anytime we want."

"Little girl want sun?" asked one troll.

"Oh, yes, please," whispered Lucia.

"Come and get it," the troll taunted, kicking a bundle of rags at Lucia. Not a gleam of light shone out of the rags. How could anything so small and shabby be the sun?

Lucia reached for the rag ball. A troll foot kicked it away. Lucia reached for the ball again. Another foot kicked it, and another, and another. Lucia stumbled through a maze of troll legs. A leg shot out in front of her.

Splunk. She fell face-down in the snow. Something hard poked at Lucia's ribs. The tinderbox!

"Wait!" Lucia cried through chattering teeth. "That ball of rags is not the sun."

"Trolls have sun!" the trolls thundered. "Trolls have sun!"

Lucia's heart beat fast, but she clambered to her knees and pulled off her mittens. She took the tinderbox from her pocket, then tried to strike a spark.

Skritch, skritch. The trolls leaned in closer. Lucia's fingers shook.

Skritch, skritch. Blue sparks skittered and died. Blue like her mother's apron. Blue like her baby brother's eyes.

Lucia struck harder. *Skritch, skritch. Skritch, skritch.*

A spark caught on the dry moss in the tinderbox. A little flame bloomed, warming Lucia's fingers, the way the fire back home used to do.

"Look!" Lucia stood and held out the box.

"I have the sun right here."

The trolls peered inside.

"That's not the sun," a troll howled, and he knocked the tinderbox from Lucia's hands. Flames sputtered across the snow and died.

"Eat her!"

"Eat her now!"

"Get sun!"

"Catch the pussums for dessert."

But the milk-white cat was quicker than the trolls. He leaped from Lucia's hood and batted the rag ball out of reach.

Faster and faster the ball rolled, rags unwinding behind it like ribbons on the snow.

"Stop! Stop!" the trolls screamed.

The last rag unrolled.

The blanket fell off.

The sun blazed forth, dazzlingly bright. Lucia covered her eyes.

CRACK!

All around Lucia, trolls turned to stone. Shadows stretched black across the snow.

Like a wheel, the sun rolled on, right off the edge of the mountaintop and up into the sky, growing bigger and brighter as it climbed. Black sky paled to rosy dawn. The mountaintops glowed.

Lucia lifted her face to the sun. Light and warmth poured over her.

Lucia picked up the little milk-white cat and kissed his fur, as silky and soft as her baby brother's hair. "Good kitty," Lucia said. "Good, good kitty."

Back down the mountain Lucia skied, through a forest of trolls and a forest of trees, the milk-white cat tucked into her hood. Her pale-blue shadow raced ahead of her.

Swoosh, swoosh. Icicles glinted and dripped and fell.

Swoosh, swoosh. Sparrows woke up and hopped in the pine branches, shaking snow on Lucia's hair.

Down and down the mountain, Lucia followed her own tracks, all the way home, where pink smoke curled from the chimney.

Sunlight followed Lucia through the front door and poured across the floor, as warm and sweet as honey. A fire blazed on the hearth, and the baby cooed and clapped to see Lucia.

"I thought I had lost you," her mother cried, sweeping Lucia into a hug. "And then the sun came up, and I knew you would come home. My brave child!"

Lucia's mother held her close. "My sunshine," she whispered. "Light of my heart."

And after breakfast, Lucia and the milk-white cat
fell fast asleep in the sunshine.